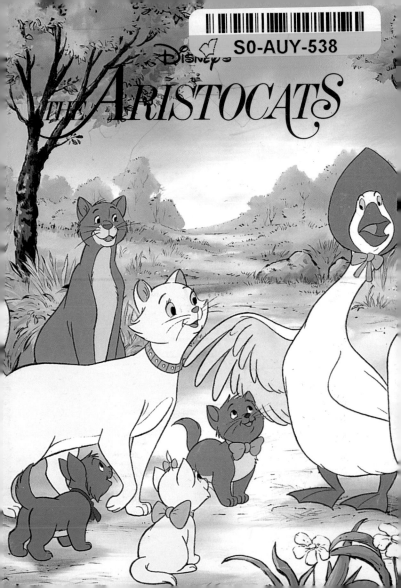

Disney's

THE ARISTOCATS

Madame Adelaide Bonfamille was a charming elderly lady who lived in Paris. She was rich, and she had no children, so instead she spoiled her cats. They were very talented cats. Berlioz could play the piano, Toulouse painted, and Marie sang. Duchess, their mother, was very proud of her kittens.

SEILA

One day, Madame Bonfamille asked her attorney to visit. "I want to make my will," she said. "Since I have no family, I shall leave everything to my cats. I am sure that Edgar, my butler, will be glad to look after them. And he will inherit my fortune when they are gone."

The lawyer agreed, and bent to kiss Madame's hand, but accidentally kissed Duchess's tail instead. They did not know that Edgar had been eavesdropping.

Edgar was furious! "I have served Madame faithfully all these years, and now she is going to leave her fortune to those cats!" he fumed.

Then he had an idea, and an evil glint lit up his eyes. That night, he stirred some sleeping pills into the cats' dinner.

The pills made Duchess and her kittens fall sound asleep. Edgar waited until Madame went to bed. Then he grabbed the cats' basket and headed for the countryside. He planned to leave the cats so far from home they would never find their way back!

But when Edgar came to a river,
two angry dogs chased after his
motorcycle. They snapped at
Edgar's legs, and he lost control of
the motorcycle. He skidded off the
road, hit a bump, and the basket
flew off the sidecar and rolled down
the riverbank. Edgar was so busy
escaping from the dogs that he
dropped the cat's basket.

Luckily, the basket stopped rolling before it landed in the river. "Where are we? Why is it so cold and dark?" the cats asked each other. To make matters worse, it started raining.

In Paris, Roquefort the mouse helped Madame Bonfamille search for the missing cats. No doubt about it, they were gone!

Morning came at last. "We're hungry," the kittens whimpered. Duchess didn't know what to do.

Then a big alley cat appeared. "My name is O'Malley," he said. "Is there anything I can do for you?"

Duchess explained their predicament.

"I know how to get to Paris!" O'Malley said.

O'Malley led the way along the railroad tracks. But a train rumbled toward them just as they were crossing a bridge. They had to leap under the tracks to hide!

The train passing overhead made a terrifying noise. So at first, no one noticed that a kitten was missing. Then Duchess cried: "Marie has fallen into the river!"

O'Malley dove bravely off the bridge and saved her.

"You are a hero!" Duchess said.

Fortunately, they had no problems
on the rest of the journey. The
kittens enjoyed the trees and
flowers and the other travelers
they met.

"Look, they have rubber feet,"
whispered Berlioz to O'Malley.

"That's because they're geese,"
O'Malley replied, chuckling.

By the time they arrived in Paris,
it was dark.

"I have an idea," said O'Malley.
"I live close by. Why don't you stay there until tomorrow?"

Duchess agreed at once. She met O'Malley's friends, who were great jazz musicians from all over the world. Duchess and her kittens danced the night away.

"What a wonderful evening," Duchess told O'Malley when the dancing had ended.

e cats
ved, Edgar

appening,
tied it up.

what

He found O'Malley outside the front door, and told him what had happened.

"I'll go help them," O'Malley said. "You go and get my friends."

O'Malley's friends made fun of Roquefort
when he showed up. But when he mentioned
O'Malley's name, they agreed to help.

In the stables, Edgar dropped the sack of cats
in a trunk. "You're going on a long voyage,"
he told them, "and then the fortune will be all
mine!" But just at that moment, O'Malley
pounced on his back.

Then O'Malley's friends arrived and took over. "Help! help! It's an army of wildcats!" Edgar yelled.

Meanwhile, O'Malley had gone to release the prisoners. Duchess looked at him gratefully. "You're always there when we need you," she said.

The butler tried to get away, but Madame Bonfamille's mare, Frou Frou, gave him a kick that sent him flying head-first into the trunk.

Edgar was still in the trunk when the movers arrived. So off he went on the long voyage he had planned for the cats.

Madame Bonfamille wept with joy when she saw her cats. "I thought I had lost you forever, my darlings," she cried. "And you, handsome young man," she said to O'Malley, "join the family. I'm going to adopt you."

"Hooray!" cried the kittens. And Duchess and O'Malley smiled lovingly at each other.